JIM SMITH
The Frog Band and the Owlnapper

LITTLE, BROWN AND COMPANY, BOSTON

Text and illustrations © 1980 by Jim Smith
Library of Congress Catalogue Card No. 80-82784
First American Edition
ISBN 0 316 80163 1
Printed in Great Britain by William Clowes (Beccles) Ltd, Beccles and London

As the family car drove him back to Peck Academy,
young Olly Hoot tapped the chauffeur on his shoulder.
"I say, Mr Hare," he said. "One of your ears has dropped off."
The chauffeur turned round, but instead of kind old Mr Hare,
it was Nick Gristle, the notorious villain!
"Keep quiet, or else," he threatened.

Meanwhile, Mr Hare had been discovered,
bound and gagged, in the kitchen at Hoot Hall.
"Young Master Olly," he gasped as Cook untied him.
"He's been owlnapped!"

Olly didn't want to go back to school,
but he surely didn't want to be owlnapped either,
so as soon as the car stopped, he jumped out.
He was not quick enough. Nick easily caught him,
and dragged him back to the car.

With a long piece of rope,
Nick tied Olly from head to claw,
and just to make sure,
he popped a clothespin over his beak.

As Nick put the trussed owl into the hamper
on the back of the car, a vanload of frogs,
on their way to the Throttle Fair, pulled up.

"Can we help?" asked Johann S. Frog,
the Frog Band leader,
but Nick only glared at them and roared off.

"What a queer chap," said Johann. "Look, he's left his hat behind!"
Shortie Frog jumped down to have a look. "He was no schoolboy.
Why was he wearing a hat with a Peck Academy badge?
Something strange is going on."

That night Nick carried his wriggling captive
in a sack to a tea wagon, high on a hill
overlooking Throttle fairground and the river.

The next day was Throttle Fair day.
The main street was full of sightseers, waiting for the parade.
They talked of nothing but Olly, the missing nephew of
Sir Octavius Hoot, the Yorkshire pudding magnate.

The parade wound its way through the town,
marching in time to the Frog Band.
Johann S. Frog proudly conducted his frogs
as they followed the Mayor of Throttle
at the head of the procession.

Nick Gristle darted across the street in front of the Mayor's car.

As he disappeared into a shop to buy pencils and paper
with which to write the ransom note,
the sharp eyes of Shortie Frog spotted him.

"Look!" he muttered to Godfrey Frog
between puffs on his tuba, "there's that badger.
The one with the car, and the hat on the road.
I bet he knows something about Olly Hoot. Come on!"
Giving his tuba to the bass drummer, he rushed after Nick.
Godfrey followed, still clutching his trombone.

Through the shop window, Nick saw them coming.
Hurriedly he climbed to the top of a stepladder and hid himself
among the buckets and pans that hung from the ceiling.
The two frogs searched the shop but never thought to look above.

Nick shifted slightly. Clang-g-g!
He hit a bucket with his elbow.
"There he is!" shouted Shortie.
But Nick pulled a tin tub from its hook and dropped it over them.
As he jumped over the trapped frogs, Nick caught his foot
in Godfrey's trombone and stumbled.

Scrambling to his feet, he escaped into the back street.
Nick ran through the alleys until he found an open door.
The bewildered clients of "Egmont's Tail Salon"
silently stared at him.

Scent bottles, chairs and jugs went flying
as he plunged through the salon
and fell down the front steps into the road.
A moment later two frogs, one waving a trombone,
blundered their way after him.

Shortie and Godfrey reached the front steps of the salon
in time to see Nick Gristle jump over a wall
and disappear from view.

Nick tumbled down the railway embankment. Sitting up,
he found himself face to face with an oncoming engine!
When the train had passed, Nick had vanished.

"It's no use, we've lost him," sighed Shortie,
but as they crossed the river to return to the parade,
Godfrey glanced down. There was Nick,
paddling across the river in a boat!
Keeping well hidden, they followed him up the hill
to the tea wagon.
"Come out. We know you're in there!"
they shouted, but there was no reply.

Inside, Olly had managed to free one claw.
When Nick came in, he tried to hop out of the door.
Nick dived to stop the little owl, and as he caught him,
he fell against the brake lever, releasing it.

The frogs decided to smoke Nick out of the wagon.
Shortie climbed up and put his hat over the stove-pipe.
The smoke blew back into the wagon,
and soon Nick could be heard coughing and spluttering.

Suddenly the skylight was flung open
and Nick appeared in a cloud of smoke.
He was trying to wrench the hat from the pipe
when Olly gave a tremendous sneeze and the pin
sprang off his beak. "Help, help, help!" he squawked.

"It's Olly!" cried the frogs.
They hurled themselves at the door, and the wagon began to move!
Gathering momentum, it rolled down the steep hill.
Horrified, the frogs saw it disappear over the edge of the hill
and fly into the air far above the fairground!

The wagon landed on the highest point of the roller coaster,
swept down the steep track, shot up the other side,
and flew on, leaving the roller coaster way behind.
In mid-air over the river, the door burst open,
Olly dropped out and fell into the chimney
of a barge beneath.

Spectators crowded the bridge as the tea wagon crashed into the water.
Nick abandoned the wagon and clung to the bridge.
Through his telescope Johann S. Frog spotted Olly.
He rallied his musicians.
"Quick now frogs, a frog chain! Over the side you go!"

The well-trained Frog Band swung over the edge,
grasping hands to ankles.

They were just able to grab Olly as the barge passed under the bridge.

"Help!" cried Nick. "I can't swim!"
A strong line of colored flags was let down,
but Nick's relief was short-lived.
He was hauled up onto the bridge
by the willing officers of the Throttle police.

Sir Octavius and Lady Hoot held a hasty press conference
on the bridge to let everyone know how grateful they were
to Johann S. Frog for saving their nephew. All had ended well
and the Frog Band found itself triumphant once again.